KAY THOMPSON'S ELOISE

Eloise's Mother's Day Surprise

STORY BY **Lisa McClatchy**

ILLUSTRATED BY **Tammie Lyon**

Ready-to-Read

Simon Spotlight
New York   London   Toronto   Sydney   New Delhi

SIMON SPOTLIGHT
An imprint of Simon & Schuster Children's Publishing Division
1230 Avenue of the Americas
New York, NY 10020
First Simon Spotlight hardcover edition March 2018
First Aladdin Paperbacks edition March 2009
Copyright © 2009 by the Estate of Kay Thompson
"Eloise" and related marks are trademarks of the Estate of Kay Thompson.
SIMON SPOTLIGHT, READY-TO-READ, and colophon are
registered trademarks of Simon & Schuster, Inc.
For information about special discounts for bulk purchases, please contact Simon & Schuster
Special Sales at 1-866-506-1949 or business@simonandschuster.com.
The text of this book was set in Century Old Style.
Manufactured in the United States of America 0218 LAK
2 4 6 8 10 9 7 5 3 1
The Library of Congress has cataloged a previous edition as follows:
Library of Congress Cataloging-in-Publication Data
McClatchy, Lisa.
Eloise's Mother's Day Surprise / story by Lisa McClatchy ;
illustrated by Tammie Lyon.—1st Aladdin Paperbacks ed.
p. cm. — (Kay Thompson's Eloise) (Ready-to-read)
Summary: Nanny takes Eloise shopping for the "best best best" Mother's Day gifts.
[1. Shopping—Fiction. 2. Gifts—Fiction. 3. Mother's Day—Fiction.
4. Plaza Hotel (New York, N.Y.—Fiction. 5. Hotels, motels, etc—Fiction.
6. New York (N.Y.)—Fiction.]
I. Lyon, Tammie, ill. II. Thompson, Kay, 1909–1998. III. Title.
PZ7.M47841375E1f 2009
[E]—dc22
2008049718
ISBN 978-1-4814-7678-2 (hc)
ISBN 978-1-4169-7889-3 (pbk)

I am Eloise.
I am six.

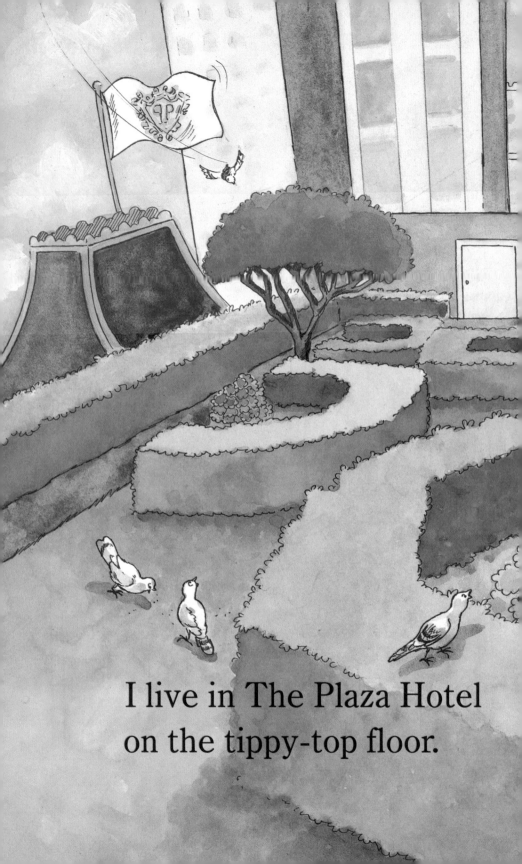

I live in The Plaza Hotel
on the tippy-top floor.

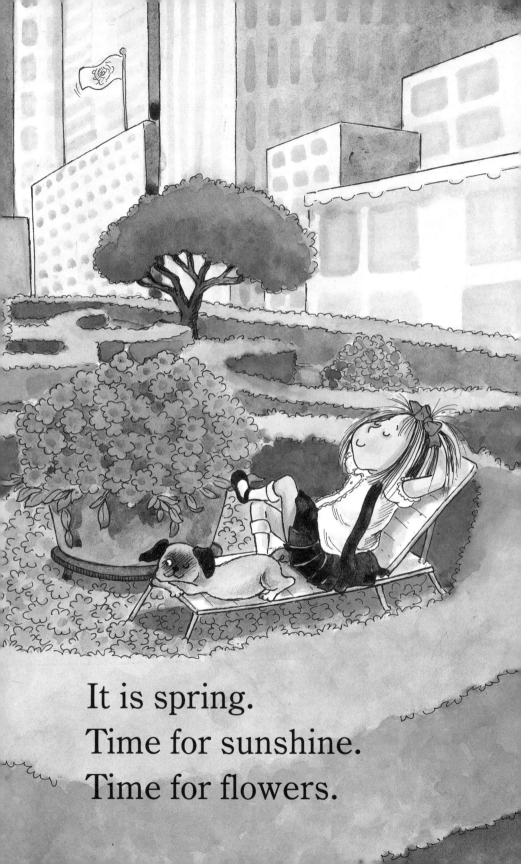

It is spring.
Time for sunshine.
Time for flowers.

Time for mothers.

Nanny says we must, must, must go shopping today. It is almost Mother's Day!

This is my dog.
His name is Weenie.

Weenie always goes
shopping with me.

We put on our sunglasses.

We put on our
springtime best.

Nanny says, "Do not forget your spring hat and your purse, Eloise!"

Oh, I love, love, love
to shop!

Nanny lets me
decide what to buy.
"First, we shall have
to buy chocolates," I say.

Weenie and I love chocolate.
So does Mother.

Nanny takes me
to Godiva.

Mother must have
the best, best, best!

"Next, we buy flowers,"
  I say to Nanny.
"This vendor will do!"

I pick the reddest roses because Mother must have the best, best, best!

"Now we shall buy her
a ring," I declare.

"Only Tiffany will do,"
I tell Nanny.
Mother must have the
best, best, best!

Only Saks Fifth Avenue
will do. Mother must have
the best, best, best!

Nanny, Weenie, and I
take our presents back
to The Plaza.

We hand them to the
manager to send them
to Mother.

"Wait, Nanny," I say
when we are done.

"I have one last thing."

"A box of chocolates for you.
And a rose."

Oh, I love, love, love, love Mother's Day!